METRO-GOLDWYN-MAYER PICTURES PRESENTS A JIM HENSON PICTURES PRODUCTION "GOOD BOY!" MOLLY SHANNON LIAM AIKEN KEVIN NEALON CO-PRODUCER BILL BANNERMAN MUSIC BY MARK MOTHERSBAUGH EDITED BY CRAIG P. HERRING PRODUCTION DESIGNER JERRY WANEK DIRECTOR OF PHOTOGRAPHY JAMES GLENNON, ASC EXECUTIVE PRODUCER STEPHANIE ALLAIN PRODUCED BY LISA HENSON KRISTINE BELSON SCREEN STORY BY ZEKE RICHARDSON AND JOHN HOFFMAN SCREENPLAY BY JOHN HOFFMAN DIRECTED BY JOHN HOFFMAN DISTRIBUTED BY MGM DISTRIBUTION CO.

www.mgm.com

GOOD BOY!: Meet the Dogs
GOOD BOY! copyright 2003 Metro-Goldwyn-Mayer Pictures Inc.
All rights reserved. Printed in the U.S.A.
Library of Congress catalog card number: 2003103701
Book design by Joe Merkel
www.harperchildrens.com

2 3 4 5 6 7 8 9 10
❖
First Edition

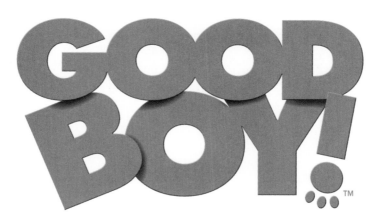

GOOD BOY!

Meet the Dogs

Adapted by Raina Moore and Kate Egan
Based on the screenplay by John Hoffman
Screen story by Zeke Richardson
and John Hoffman

HarperFestival®
A Division of HarperCollins*Publishers*

Meet the dogs!

Fluffy dogs and skinny dogs.

Brown dogs and spotted dogs.

Some dogs are tall.

Some dogs are short.

Some dogs like to look pretty.

Hello, Barbara Ann!

Ms. Ryan is Barbara Ann's owner.

She treats Barbara Ann like a queen.

This is Shep.

He is big, but he is never mean.

Shep is Connie's best friend.
Shep loves Connie so much that he
gives her sloppy, wet kisses!

Some dogs are brave.

Nelly is not one of them.

Nelly is even afraid of the news!

She only likes the comics.

Wilson is one cool dog.

He loves to play catch.

He also loves to eat!

Wilson wishes he could use a can opener.

These dogs are all friends.

They walk together every day.

Owen is their dog-walker.

Owen has his own dog, too.

His dog's name is Hubble.

Hubble is not like other dogs.

He is from outer space!

Hubble came from Sirius, the Dog Star.

He flew to Earth in a spaceship.

Hubble can talk!

The other dogs don't like

what he says.

He tells them they are silly.

He tells them they are lazy.

Why does Hubble say these things?

Hubble is a dog on a mission.

On his planet, dogs are in charge.

Hubble thinks they should be in charge
on Earth, too.

He will get the Earth dogs into shape!

No more playing tricks.

No more wearing clothes.

Hubble doesn't like leashes.

He thinks the humans should be walked!

Hubble can't stand dog bowls.

He says dinner belongs on fancy dishes!

Hubble is strict with the other dogs.

Too bad he can't stick to his own rules.

He isn't supposed to act like

an Earth dog.

But Hubble does like having his belly

scratched, and he loves playing catch!

Hubble is surprised when this dog shows up.

Her name is the Greater Dane.

She is very powerful—

and very scary.

This dog is scary, too.

He is the Greater Dane's sidekick.

Don't let his size fool you!

These dogs also come from Sirius.
They want to see how Hubble
has helped the Earth dogs.

They do not like what they see!

Hubble has not changed
Earth dogs at all.

Hubble has become just like them!
Hubble likes his new friends,
and he is going to stay.